THE SECRET JUNGLE

ADAM BLADE

ORCHARD

MEET TEAM HERO ...

POWER: Super-strength

LIKES: Ventura City FC

DISLIKES: Bullies

RUBY
POWER: Fire vision
LIKES: Comic books
DISLIKES: Small spaces
DANNY
POWER: Super-hearing, able to generate sonic blasts
LIKES: Pizza
DISLIKES: Thunder

CONTENTS

PROLOGUE	9
INTO THE JUNGLE	15
TEMPLE DESTRUCTION	29
BLOOD TRAIL	45
A TIGHT SQUEEZE	61
HOSTAGE	75
BATTLE AGAINST BORTUS	87
THE HIDDEN CLUE	105

PROLOGUE

THE SCREEN read, "You have an incoming video call from Dr Heather Jabari."

Ruby grinned. Her mother had been on an expedition deep in the jungle for the last year, and getting messages there was tricky. She pressed the "answer" tab, and her mum's face filled the monitor. She was in some sort of large canvas structure, with a mosquito net hanging above her.

"Hey, Rubes! Sorry it's been so long, sweetheart! We've been incredibly busy here. How are things going at Hero Academy?""

"Oh, y'know, crazy! Like always!" Ruby didn't often go into details about all their dangerous missions. *No need to scare Mum ...*

"I bet. And your friends? Jack, wasn't it? And the boy with the bat ears ... Donny."

"Danny!" said Ruby. "They're all good." She paused. "So, will you be home for the holidays this year?"

Her mum made a sad face. "Oh, darling, I really don't know yet. We're making lots of progress here at the Taah Lu site. We thought we'd finished with the temple excavation, but then we found a secret chamber under one end. We had to be careful – didn't want to risk causing a collapse. But it was worth it! We discovered a rather fascinating stone carving under there. We're still working on the translation of the symbols, because the language is not one I've seen before – but we think it's talking about some sort of weapon."

"Sounds dangerous," said Ruby.

"Ha! Not really. It's thousands of years old, but it's still fascinating. In fact, we think that—"

The sound of an explosion suddenly ripped through the speakers. It was loud enough to make the image on the screen shake and cause Ruby to flinch in her seat.

"What on earth was that?" asked Dr Jabari. She swivelled her head to look at something off screen.

Another burst of sound – gunfire, maybe – crackled distantly. Rips appeared in the canvas.

"Mum!" said Ruby in horror. "Mum, what's happening?"

On the screen, her mother looked up anxiously as a man burst through the mosquito net. He was bleeding from a cut on the head. "Dr Jabari – we're under attack! We've got to get out! I think they're after the—"

The screen went black.

CHAPTER 1

INTO THE JUNGLE

IN THE Hero Academy Command Centre, the main monitor had been playing Dr Jabari's message on loop for the last ten minutes. Jack watched carefully, while also keeping an eye on his friend, Ruby. Danny had an arm around her shoulders. Though she was obviously upset, her eyes glinted with determination. Jack's heart ached for her. He knew what it was like to see your parents in danger.

Also standing before the bank of terminals and screens were Chancellor Rex, the Academy's head, and their tutors, Professor Rufus and Professor Yokata. All of them looked deeply concerned.

Ruby slammed a hand on the control panel, pausing the footage.

"We've got to do something!" she said.

Professor Yokata nodded. "And we will, Ruby," she said. "Though we have to know what we're dealing with first."

"Where is this Taah Lu temple Dr. Jabari was investigating?" asked Jack.

"The Parracudo Jungle," said Chancellor Rex. "One of the last great wildernesses on our planet. The Taah Lu were an ancient civilisation who stood against the High Command's attacks."

"They fought General Gore?" asked Danny.

The Chancellor shook his head. "This was long before the era of Noxx. We're not sure exactly what happened, but about five thousand years ago they were almost completely wiped out."

"By this 'weapon' Ruby's mum mentioned?" asked Jack.

"Perhaps," said Rex. "If there's any chance it will come to light again, we have to stop it."

"It will be very risky," said Professor Rufus. "Parts of the Parracudo Jungle are completely unmapped. Anything could be lurking in there."

"Who cares?" snapped Ruby. "We have to rescue my mum!"

Chancellor Rex took a deep breath, closing his eyes and lifting his hands in front of him so the palms faced one another. Jack had seen him using his special power several times, but it never ceased to be amazing. Their head teacher could create visions of the future.

Between his hands, the air blurred with an image of what looked like a modern city of gleaming skyscrapers. But almost at once, metal flashed across the sky, cutting into the buildings like shrapnel, causing bursts of flame and plumes of smoke. Jack heard terrified screams as the great towers began to fold in on themselves and crash to the ground. The vision filled with debris and dust and black clouds, then faded away.

Chancellor Rex, his head beading with sweat, lowered his arms. His skin was pale. "I don't know what it means," he muttered.

"Well, it certainly didn't look good," said Danny.

"So what are we waiting for?" asked Ruby, fixing their teachers with a fierce glare.

"The only place we'll get answers is in the Parracudo Jungle," said Jack. "Come on – let's go!"

• • •

With Professor Yokata piloting, Jack sat beside his friends in the hold of *Arrow III*, the Academy's private jet.

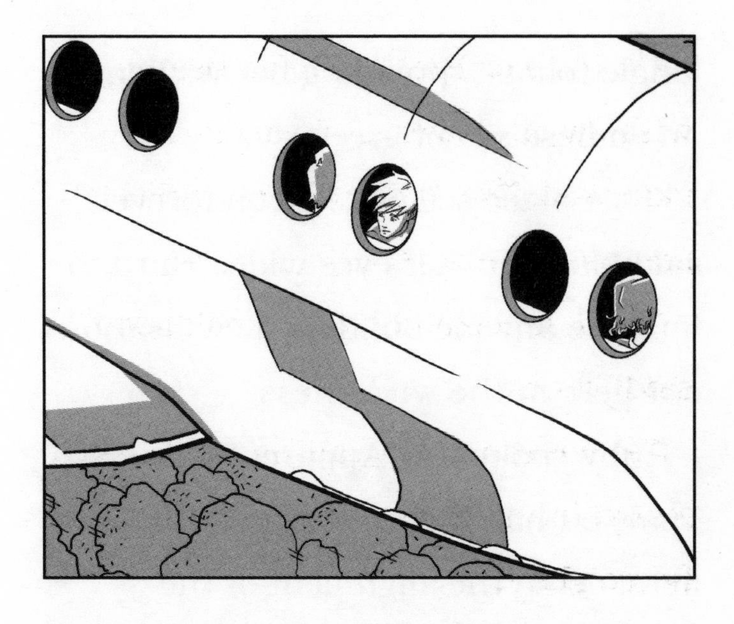

Ruby had barely spoken since they left, but stared blankly ahead. Danny was somehow managing to sleep. Across the other side were two older students Yokata had selected for the mission – Madison and Simon. Through the windows, Jack saw jungle foliage spreading below them in an endless sea of greenery.

"This place seems to go on forever!" said Madison, her eyes wide. "Hard to imagine anyone building a civilisation out here in the wilderness."

Ruby spoke up. "Apparently the Taah Lu had built several cities out here, using the alignment of the stars as a guide. They flourished for almost a thousand years, but then they died out. No one knows quite how many crumbled buildings lie under the jungle canopy, nor why the Taah Lu disappeared. But the myths tell of another race who had made war against them."

"Wow – you know a lot about these guys," said Simon.

Ruby looked a little sad. "Mum's studied them her whole life."

Jack patted her on the arm. "We'll find her, Ruby," he promised – though, looking at the millions of acres of jungle below, he wondered how easy that would be.

A needle in a haystack might be easier ...

"We're almost at the temple site," said Yokata. "Get ready to disembark."

"Hey, wake up, Danny," said Jack to his gently snoring friend.

Danny didn't stir, but from the other side of the hold, Simon reached out an arm. His limb stretched unnaturally, like it was made of rubber, until it was over three metres long. Jack still found himself surprised when he saw another

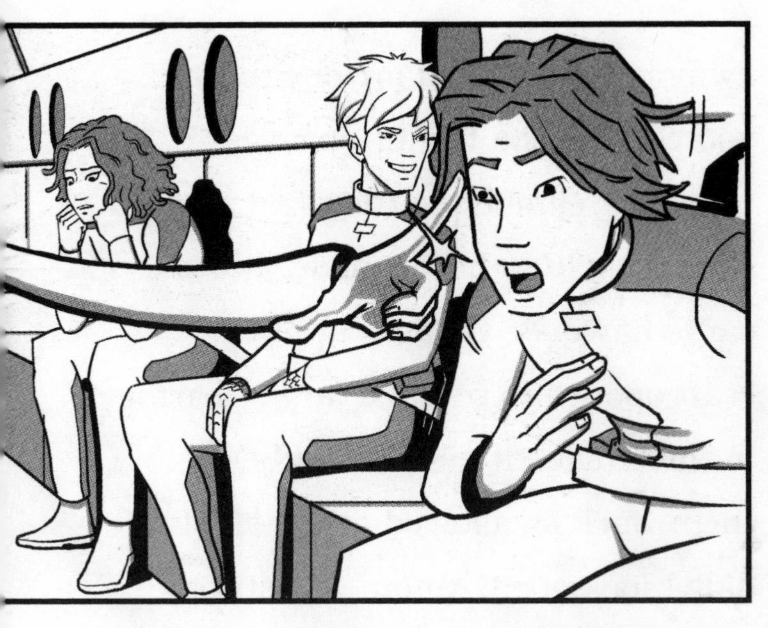

student's power for the first time. Simon flicked Danny's bat-like ear.

"Hey ... What ... Where ... ?" said Danny, sitting bolt upright.

Simon smiled. "We're here, big ears," he said with a wink.

Danny swatted the skinny arm

away playfully. "Did anyone tell you, you could use a few bicep curls?"

As they climbed to their feet, Yokata set *Arrow III* to hover mode, and the cargo bay door at the rear of the craft opened to reveal a large clearing in the jungle, fifteen metres below them. Jack swallowed at the sight. It didn't look good. Among the stubby sand-coloured remains of walls and columns and archaeological trenches, smoke rose from smouldering equipment and tents. A satellite transmitter array was smashed to pieces. Ruby gasped, her hand going to her mouth.

What happened here? Jack wondered.

Danny's ears suddenly pricked. "Guys, I think I hear—" He was interrupted by the jet's alarms.

"Sensors detect we're being targeted by a weapons system!" yelled Yokata. "Eyes sharp!"

And then Jack saw it. Near the tree line, some sort of metal tower was bristling like a tree trunk sprouting buds the size of apples. The top three began to detach, hovering in the air for a moment like floating grenades.

Then they shot towards *Arrow III*.

"Missiles incoming!" Jack shouted.

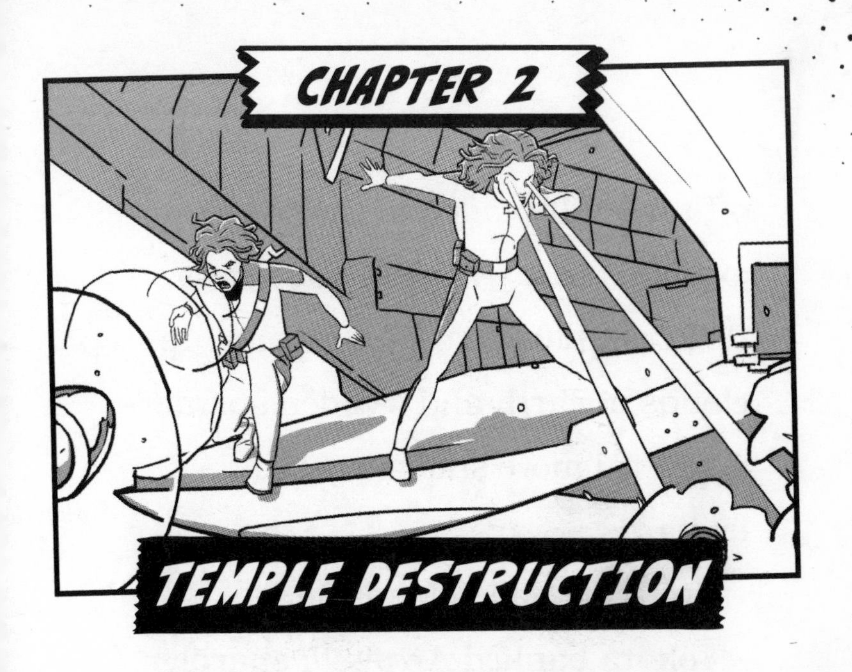

STANDING AT the open bay door, Ruby scorched the air with fire-beams from her eyes. She zapped the first two flying spheres, which dropped away like flaming comets. But the third came right at them. Danny opened his mouth and delivered a sonic blast, which knocked the sphere off target. It landed in the trees and exploded in a strangely soundless flicker of blue sparks, throwing up clouds of earth and wooden splinters.

Several more spheres arced upwards.

"Retreat!" called Madison.

Yokata banked *Arrow III* sharply and climbed, throwing them all off balance. The deadly globes rose in pursuit. Ruby steadied herself and shot her fire-beams again in a wide arc. Danny sent out more blasts, intercepting the swarm of spheres. But they continued to detach from their launch tower and sped towards the craft. Jack wished he could help, but at this range neither his super-strong hands nor Blaze, his sunsteel sword, were of any use.

One of the round silver charges slipped past a fire-beam and caught one of *Arrow*'s wings. The jet shook with an explosion and shrill alarms went off as blue sparks spread over the wing. *It's interfering with the electrical signals*, Jack realised. He'd never seen tech like it. The hold was filling with smoke. And more spheres were on their way. Ruby kept firing, and Danny kept yelling, but Jack could tell that it was no good. *There are just too many*.

"We need to abandon ship!" he cried.

"Auto-stabilising!" said Yokata through the intercom. A second later, she emerged from the cockpit, already drawing her blaster pistols and taking out two orbs with her unfailing aim. Jack knew they didn't have long before they were overwhelmed, though. Another sphere connected with *Arrow*'s fuselage, ripping a hole through it, and then detonating silently, throwing blue spinning lights across the interior. Danny stumbled and fell towards the open bay doors, but Madison caught him just in time.

Zap! Zap! Zap! Professor Yokata was taking the spheres out as quickly as she could pull the trigger.

"I'll cover you!" she cried. "Get to the jungle canopy! You can shelter underneath the branches."

Jack saw she was right. *It's the only way*. But the trees were a long way down.

Simon was fastening a harness around his middle. At first, Jack wondered what he was even doing, but then he watched in astonishment as the older boy stretched out both arms, letting them grow and grow until he could grip the uppermost branches of a nearby tree. With his body braced by the harness, his arms were like a zip-wire between the jet and the canopy.

"Go!" he said. "Use my arms!"

Ruby's flames downed another deadly silver orb.

Zap! Zap! went Yokata's blaster. More missiles were coming.

"We need to take out that weapons tower!" said Jack. Ruby nodded, and directed her fire-beam right at the base of the jutting missile turret. It began to glow orange, then red as the metal began to melt.

Danny went first from the craft,

climbing hand over hand, dangling from Simon's arm.

"You next!" Jack said to Madison.

She nodded and clambered down, joining Danny in the treetops.

Jack went third. He tried to ignore

the silver spheres as they exploded under Yokata's fire. The turret below began to groan, then tilt under Ruby's assault.

As Jack jumped into the canopy, another of the strange explosives hit the plane. The craft listed dangerously, and Simon grimaced as he held on, limbs stretched close to breaking point. The launch tower finally gave way, toppling into the tree, and Ruby's fire-beams sputtered out. Jack would have cheered, but there were still spheres spinning towards them through the air. Ruby made her way along the arms next, and Jack helped her on to the branch beside him. More spheres found their target, and the blue sparks overwhelmed the plane. The smoke was now so thick around Yokata, Jack could barely see her. Then Simon was swinging towards them.

Jack gasped. *His harness must have come loose!*

Danny snapped out an arm to catch him and haul him into the treetop.

The older boy looked back towards the jet, as it turned nose-down in the sky, the stabilisers giving out.

Yokata ...

"Hold my waist!" shouted Simon.

Jack gripped him, letting the strength of his golden hands glow. Simon's arm stretched again, and he shot out a hand towards the plane's smoke-filled hold as *Arrow III* fell through the air. A moment later, Yokata burst out of the smoke, clutching Simon's hand, her face smeared with soot and coughing violently. Jack braced to help Simon lift her towards them. As she found her feet in the uppermost branches, the group watched the craft crash into the jungle with a *whoomph* of smoke. There was no explosion, only a horrible silence.

"I guess we'd better start work on *Arrow IV* then," said Danny.

A few of the party smiled, but no one was really in a joking mood.

They picked their way down through the jungle canopy, using a combination of Simon's reach and Jack's strength to lower each other, branch by branch, to safety. On the ground, bruised and scratched, the mission team crossed the undergrowth towards the archaeological site, using Yokata's Oracle for guidance. On the edge of the clearing, they came to the collapsed missile turret.

"Is this the weapon Dr Jabari was talking about?" asked Madison.

They pressed closer, and Professor Yokata crouched beside the turret. Its surface was a smooth metal. "I don't think so," she said. "This is modern

tech, but the weapon the inscription talked about must have been as ancient as the Taah Lu themselves."

Jack saw that where the turret had broken under Ruby's fire-beams there was some sort of metallic liquid seeping out. It looked like the mercury in a thermometer.

"What is that, Hawk?" he asked his Oracle.

"Initiating chemical analysis," said Hawk.

"There's more shining gloop in these," said Danny. He had picked up one of the missiles. It had a transparent shell, and as Danny tipped it, the silver liquid inside sloshed thickly.

"Is it an explosive?" said Simon.

Hawk spoke up. ***"The composition is not one in my databanks."***

"Is that your way of saying you don't know something?" asked Jack.

"I will continue to process ..."

"Don't touch it," Professor Yokata warned. "It could be toxic."

Ruby pressed on into the clearing, stepping round the shreds of a tent towards the remains of the temples. A few vine-covered columns and part of the roof were still there.

"Hello?" Ruby called. She clutched

her mirrored shield. "Mum?"

Professor Yokata followed with her blasters. Jack drew Blaze, just in case. Danny unslung his energy bow.

Inside the temple, there was more smashed electrical equipment, and even the half-eaten remains of a foodpack. Jack remembered the scary footage. *Whatever hit Dr Jabari's team, it was fast, and completely unexpected.*

Danny's head jerked around, and he pointed to a fallen column. The space behind was a dark recess.

"I hear breathing," he said, readying his crossbow. "There's someone there!"

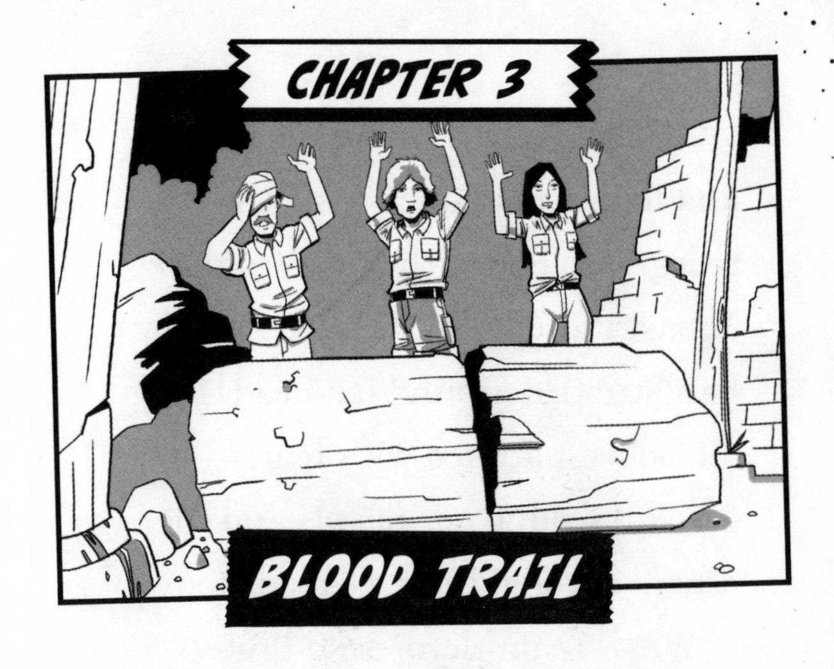

"COME OUT," said Yokata, levelling a pistol in the direction of the sound.

Two hands emerged, held straight up, and a voice echoed through the ruins. "Please, don't hurt us. We're just scientists."

The figures stood up – two men and a woman, each dressed in khakis and light shirts. Jack instantly recognised one of the men from Dr Jabari's recording. He had a grubby bandage tied around his head. They all looked haunted with fear.

Yokata slung her pistols and the others lowered their weapons too.

"We're Team Hero," said Professor Yokata.

"Thank goodness!" said the bandaged man. "I'm Dr Eric Gruber. And these are my colleagues, Dr Sochi and Dr Kim."

"Where's my mum?" asked Ruby. Dr Gruber looked confused. "'Dr Jabari," Ruby made clear.

The three scientists looked at one another. "I'm afraid," said Dr Sochi, "she was taken."

"Taken by who?" asked Ruby.

"We were attacked the day after we found the strange Taah Lu inscription," said Dr Gruber. "The man – if he was a man – he took the stone tablet on which the inscription was carved, and your mother as well. We couldn't stop him. We have no weapons, and he was colossal. When we tried to give chase, that tower attacked us with its bombs. All we could do was hide."

"Which way did he take her?" asked

Ruby. Jack could see from the sparks in her eyes that she was ready to fight, however mysterious or daunting their foe.

Dr Gruber raised a trembling finger and pointed off into the jungle. "That way ..."

"Right!" said Ruby, and she began to head off in that direction.

Professor Yokata caught her arm. "Wait, Ruby! We need to be cautious. That turret almost killed us. We're dealing with an enemy unlike any we've met before. The key to winning a war is understanding your foe."

"We can't just sit around talking!"

snapped Ruby, tugging her arm free.

Jack moved into her path. "I think what the Professor is saying is that we should gather intelligence first."

Ruby breathed a slow breath. "I know ... You're right," she said with a nod.

"Dr Jabari said the stone tablet mentioned something about a weapon," said Danny. "Can you tell us anything about that?"

Dr Gruber gestured for them to follow and strode across the temple floor. "Not a lot," he said. "We found the stone tablet in a secret chamber. Down there."

Jack saw there was a small hole in the ground, with a ladder leading inside. Gruber reached into his jacket and pulled out what looked like a smartphone. He pressed a few buttons and a hologram sprang to life above it. "This is a 3D scan we took of the stone tablet before it was stolen." Everyone peered closer as the object slowly rotated. It was a slab of stone, only perhaps thirty centimetres across and three centimentres thick. Its surface was covered in tightly packed etchings that looked a little like mathematical symbols, though there were also pictograms of trees, birds and cats, and of swirling lines, stars and crescent moons. Across the middle was a curving, irregular line like a coiling snake, with three dots at random intervals along its edge. The images at the bottom showed ranks of warriors holding spears facing a row of tall opponents wearing flowing robes.

"Is that supposed to be a battle of some sort?" asked Madison.

"We really don't know," said Dr Gruber, "but we think the spear bearers are the Taah Lu."

"Wait, zoom in on their enemies," said Jack. Dr Gruber adjusted the image, and Jack pointed at a tall soldier's hands. "He's got six fingers!"

"Weird," said Danny.

Jack asked Hawk for any records relating to six-fingered soldiers, but the Oracle couldn't tell him anything.

He heard Ruby moan, and turned around to see she had drifted a few metres away. She was holding a small video camera, its lens smashed and its casing cracked open. "This was Mum's," she said.

"Is that how you chatted?" asked Madison. "Maybe it kept recording after the transmission ended?"

Ruby came back over, and turned

the screen to face them. She pressed play, and the message began.

"Hey, Rubes! Sorry it's been so..."

Ruby fast-forwarded through the rest of their conversation, and Jack could see she was holding her breath.

As the footage played again, it showed smoke clearing and Dr Jabari being lifted into the air by her neck by a huge man. Or maybe not a man at all. He was at least two metres tall, his body bulging unnaturally with enormous muscles. *He looks like something from a cartoon ...* Maybe it was the corrupted footage, but his veins seemed to glitter oddly.

"Mum!" Ruby cried. "Oh, Mum, no..."

"Where is the stone tablet with the inscription?" growled the man.

Though hoisted over the man's colossal shoulder, Ruby's mother was scrabbling at a shelving unit with rows of tagged archaeological finds, and her fingers closed on a pen. She drove its tip into the arm holding her, and the giant yelped and let her go. Dr Jabari scrambled away, and the giant turned towards the camera. He reached out and picked it up. His hand closed over the lens, and the screen went dark.

"She's filming this," he said.

"It doesn't matter," said another

voice, dry and mechanical-sounding, almost robotic. "We have the stone tablet. Find her, Bortus. We need her to translate if we're to find the—"

The camera blurred as it was

thrown across the room. And then the recording stopped.

"Do you think they caught her?" asked Ruby, her lip quivering.

At first, Jack didn't know what to say. He'd never seen such a terrifying person as Bortus. "I don't know," he managed to mumble, then added quickly, "but it sounded like they needed your mother for something."

"We'll get her back," said Danny, looking determined.

"Who was that man?" asked Jack.

"Bortus," said Yokata, shaking her head. "We were schoolfriends."

"Friends?" everyone said at once.

The Professor nodded. "We started at the Academy in the same year. Bortus was amazing. He had the power to shapeshift his hands into any form he wanted. But he was always getting into trouble. Eventually he was expelled. He disappeared underground for several years, becoming a criminal for hire. Seems like he's got a new boss."

"So what's going on with his skin?" asked Danny. "It almost looked like his veins had that same liquid from the missiles, but inside him. Bortus is human, right?"

"He was," said Professor Yokata. "I'm

not sure what he's become ..."

What's that supposed to mean? Jack wondered. Then he noticed something on the ground. "Dr Jabari might have given us the best shot at defeating him, though."

"With that pen?" asked Simon. "I think it will take more than that."

Jack crouched down and pointed to a blob of silvery liquid. "Whether she meant to or not, she laid a trail."

"Bortus's blood!" said Ruby. She ran a few steps, to where another spatter had hit a collapsed stone. "All we have to do is follow it."

"Madison, Simon," said Professor

Yokata, "you and I will stay here with the scientists in case Bortus and his boss come back. See if you can fix up a communication array to contact the Academy Command Centre so we can give them an update."

"What shall we do?" asked Danny.

Ruby was already running to the next silver droplets, on a tree trunk three metres away. "We're going to find my mum!" she said.

BORTUS'S TRAIL led back into the trees and wasn't always easy to follow. But every time it looked like it had run out, one of them found another trace of the strange silvery substance.

The undergrowth grew so dense Jack had to draw Blaze in order to hack through. Above, in the canopy, he caught flashes of bright-feathered birds, and the occasional small monkey leaping between the branches.

"Ouch!" said Danny, slapping his neck. "I hate mosquitoes!"

"At least you're keeping them away from us," said Ruby. "Wait," she said, pausing a few paces ahead. Jack and Danny drew up alongside her. "This drop's all smeared."

She was right. It looked almost like something had tried to brush the markings away.

"Maybe they're trying to cover their tracks," said Danny. He peered ahead.

"Anyone see where the trail goes?"

"I can help," said Hawk, in Jack's ear. ***"The substance might be unknown to modern science, but it's giving off a faint energy signature. Head to eleven o'clock, twelve paces."***

Jack took the lead, following Hawk's directions. And there it was – the next drop. This one had been almost entirely wiped away.

"Scanning," said Hawk, then ***"Fourteen paces, straight ahead."***

They continued in the same direction and found the next smear, then the next. The air under the canopy was so humid that Jack's clothes were soaked through. Worse still, he had the horrible feeling they were being led into some sort of trap.

"Stop!" whispered Ruby.

Jack did as she said, and turned around. She was looking above him, her eyes wide. Jack tilted his head back and saw a huge snake – a python, if he wasn't mistaken – wrapped around a low branch, mostly hidden by leaves. Its head dangled down. Jack's heart skipped a beat.

Then the snake dropped, jaws gaping for his face. Jack threw up his free hand, and the snake bit down. Jack tried to pull free, but the snake's thick, mottled coils were already wrapping around his body. His hand glowed gold, preventing the snake's fangs from penetrating his skin, but the reptile wasn't letting go.

"Help me!" said Jack, as the snake slid around his legs.

"Your elevated heart rate indicates fear of poisoning," said Hawk. ***"But your concern is misplaced. This snake is not venomous."***

"Good," said Jack.

"It's a constrictor," said Hawk. ***"It kills by grabbing and crushing its victims."***

"Oh, great," said Jack, "that makes me feel so much better."

Danny and Ruby were grabbing at the scaled body, pulling desperately.

"It's too strong!" said Danny.

Jack lost his footing and fell to the ground. The snake was sliding around

his neck, but he dropped his sword and managed to get another hand between the creature and his throat. He gritted his teeth and pushed with all his strength. For a second the grip loosened, but then the snake's eyes glittered silver and it seemed to strangle him with even greater power.

How can it be this strong?

"What's up with its eyes?" asked Danny.

"Stand back!" said Ruby. She shot a stream of fire at the snake's thickly muscled body, but as soon as it connected, a silver sheen spread from the point of impact. The snake didn't even flinch.

"Bortus's blood is protecting it somehow!" said Danny.

"Fascinating," said Hawk. ***"If at all possible, we should take a sample back to the Academy."***

"Yeah ... it's really awesome," choked Jack. "Any other ideas about, y'know, helping me?"

Danny picked up Blaze. "We could try this." He angled the point at the python's body and stabbed hard, but the snake's skin clanged like metal.

Jack felt like he was being crushed by the world's strongest man.

The snake let go of his hand, its head rearing back as if ready to strike. But before it could lash out, Ruby grabbed its neck and yanked the other way. The snake bucked in her grip, and each spasm made it tighten around Jack. Any more, and he feared his bones would shatter.

Then the snake began to drag him across the ground. Its head tore free of Ruby's grasp, its attention shifting to something deeper into the jungle. The snake pulsed through the undergrowth with Jack still wrapped in its coils.

Where is it taking me?

Suddenly the snake stopped. Lying on his side, Jack saw they were beside a small pool of the silvery substance. The python dipped its head and lapped it up greedily. Waves of silver shimmered along its length.

"Looks like it's addicted to that stuff," said Danny.

Jack felt the creature's grip loosen a bit, and the snake's scales began to harden under his fingers, almost like the giant reptile was stiffening from within. As it consumed the silver goo, he managed to prise away the coils near his neck.

“It’s getting weaker!” he said. “Help me!”

His friends joined the struggle, taking hold of different sections of the snake and bracing themselves against the jungle floor. As the snake licked at the puddle, they succeeded in pulling away the remaining coils enough for Jack to scramble free. He stood up, flexing his arms. When he looked back at his attacker, he saw the snake had changed almost completely. Its whole body had become silvered and stiff like a sculpture made of polished metal. It shifted a little, but when its tongue flickered again, it seemed to be in slow motion. And though it moved towards them, eyes glinting, Jack stepped aside easily.

"It's eaten too much!" said Ruby. "The metal's overwhelmed its body."

Danny crouched beside the snake and peered at its scales. "Not so tough now, are you?"

"It could wake up at any time," said Jack. He glanced up. The light was fading. "It'll be night soon – we need to keep moving. Hawk, can you still follow the trail?"

"Two o'clock. Fifteen paces."

They left the snake behind, and forged on through the jungle undergrowth. The patches of silver here were untouched by the snake and easier to find. It wasn't long before they saw a faint tinge of strange blue light ahead. They slowed their steps, trying to place each foot with care.

Jack had no idea what was waiting for them, but he wasn't optimistic. Just a few drops of the silvery goo had made the snake deadly … and Bortus had the stuff flowing through his veins!

This is not going to be an easy fight …

CHAPTER 5

HOSTAGE

AS THE trees thinned, Jack saw the blue light was coming from several bulbs that stood like stout streetlamps around the perimeter of an encampment. The jungle floor was flattened under a metal base platform, and several low domes, also metal-plated, stood dotted over the ground. It looked to Jack like the sort of base you'd find on the moon or in a sci-fi movie, all smooth lines and glowing surfaces.

Jack lifted his finger to his lips.

"Hawk," he whispered. "Can you detect any security systems?"

"Scanning ..." said his Oracle. ***"There are motion sensors, which I can deactivate remotely."***

"Do it," said Jack.

They crept into the camp, and Jack heard a voice. Straight away he recognised it from the recording of the kidnap – mechanical, like it was being filtered through a speaker.

"You've lost a lot of Xanthrum, Bortus," the voice said. "It doesn't grow on trees, you know."

"Sorry, boss," replied Bortus, in his gravelly tone. "She put up a fight."

Jack peered around the edge of one of the low buildings. Under an awning, Bortus was reclining on a gurney, bathed in blue light. Jack was still unnerved by the man's size – like a normal human body had been inflated, his skin stretched over swollen muscles. Standing over him was a tall, thin man, wearing a strange robe that gleamed like metal but looked flexible, falling in folds. It reminded Jack of medieval chain mail, but he sensed it was high-tech and lightweight. The man's face was covered by a silver mask with empty eye sockets, and some sort of grille over his mouth. In a gauntleted hand he held something that looked like a ray-gun, which he pressed to the upper part of Bortus's arm.

"This might hurt a bit. Hold still."

He depressed the trigger with a hissing sound and Bortus spasmed on the bed, crying out in pain. Jack saw the threads of silver pulsing into his veins. *Xanthrum?*

'Don't be such a baby,' said the other man. *If he's a doctor*, Jack thought, *he doesn't have a great bedside manner*.

"Is that all I get?" asked Bortus, sitting up and rolling his head on his muscular neck.

"Remember the deal," said his boss. "When I have what I want, you get all the Xanthrum you could ever need."

"I helped you get the Taah Lu inscription, didn't I?" said Bortus sulkily.

The tall man standing over him

growled. "Sadly, much knowledge of the old tongue has been lost. I need to know the secrets of the inscription if I'm to unlock its power."

"She has the knowledge," said Bortus, with a toss of his head. "World-famous expert, aren't you?"

"And I'll never reveal it to either of you," mumbled a female voice.

That's Ruby's mum!

Ruby gasped, and Jack grabbed her arm to stop her running out.

They moved silently a few more paces, until the rest of the camp's interior came into view. Ruby's mum was seated on the ground, her hands tied in front of her.

"Brave words," the tall man said, turning to face her. "But I won't let a puny human stand in my way."

Does that mean he's not human? Jack wondered.

"Well, this is what we puny humans call a stalemate," said Ruby's mum.

A synthesised laughter seeped through the grille. "Perhaps I wasn't clear, Dr Jabari. I need that weapon. Bortus, make her talk."

"With pleasure," said his henchman, standing up from the gurney and holding out his right hand. The veins of his arm bulged like silvered cords under his skin, and his hand began to change. His fingers flooded with metallic colouring. Jack swallowed, remembering what Professor Yokata had said about his power. Before his eyes, the fingers joined and swelled to become a spinning drillbit. On the ground, Dr Jabari tried to press herself back against the wall, her face full of fear.

"That's impossible!" she said.

"That's the power of Xanthrum," said Bortus. He stalked towards her, drill spinning. "Tell me, where's the weapon my master wants?"

Dr Jabari fixed him with a hard

stare. "I won't tell you anything," she said.

Bortus brought the drill close to her face.

Ruby, unable to hold back any

longer, tore free from Jack's grip and shot a fire-beam. It slammed into Bortus's side, blasting him back a metre or so. Jack and Danny ran out from hiding too.

"Ruby!" cried Dr Jabari.

But the man in the cloak grabbed her, pulling her towards him, then began to run away. Danny aimed an energy bolt at the cloaked man, and fired. The aim was perfect, but their enemy shot vertically upwards on some sort of invisible jetpack. As he did so, he tapped something at his wrist; moments later, the buildings of the base began to collapse in on themselves like a falling structure of playing cards. The outer walls folded upwards too, locking into one another. It was some kind of giant cage and as the seals suctioned into place, Jack and his friends found themselves trapped inside. With Bortus. Glowing seams in the metal plating lit the scene with soft blue light.

The brutish giant grinned, and Jack saw that even his teeth were coated in the silver Xanthrum.

His drillbit was still spinning. "Team Hero," he said. "At school, I always liked sparring. But practice time is over. Now, you three are going to die."

CHAPTER 6

BATTLE AGAINST BORTUS

JACK DREW Blaze while Ruby lowered her shield in front of her. Danny released another bolt from his crossbow but Bortus raised a hand, which morphed into a metal disc, and the charge bounced off harmlessly. Jack leapt at him, swinging his sword.

Bortus caught the blade in a metal hand, sending a tremor of pain into Jack's shoulder.

With a twist, Bortus ripped the sword away and threw it aside. Jack balled his scaled hand into a fist, driving it into Bortus's midsection.

The blow struck with a dull metal *clang*.

"Been working on my abs," said Bortus, grinning. He clamped a hand around Jack's throat and lifted him off the ground. Ruby came running in from the other side, but Bortus swung a metal fist. It lengthened into a pole, catching her legs and sweeping her off

her feet. Then he hurled Jack away, and he crashed into the inner wall of the pod. Danny came to Jack's side.

"You OK?"

"Not really," said Jack. "How do we

fight a guy made of metal?"

Bortus pressed a button on his wrist and his chest swelled. The veins across his torso glowed bright silver, and his eyes flickered. "Ah – that's better," said the giant.

He's giving himself a Xanthrum boost, Jack realised.

Both Bortus's hands then changed shape, each becoming a chain ending in a spiked mace. He began to swing them around, like deadly wrecking balls. One direct hit would easily cave their skulls in.

"We need to get out of this cage!" said Danny, as their enemy paced towards them. Jack turned and drove a punch into the wall behind him. It left a fist-shaped dent, but the wall held firm. He thought he could break through after a few more punches, but they didn't have time. They needed to get out of here now.

"Look out!" cried Ruby.

Jack turned to see one of Bortus's maces flying towards him. He ducked, the spiked ball whizzing over his head.

That was close!

Danny stepped forward and released a sonic blast that made Bortus stagger backwards – but the reverberation rebounded off the walls, and thumped into Jack. He fell to his knees, clasping his hands over his ears.

Bortus advanced on them.

"Headache? Let me see if I can help." He swung the mace. It whistled past Jack and sank into the metal wall with a dull thud. As Bortus tore it free again, the panel sheared open with a screech. It wasn't a big enough gap to slip through, but it was an opening Jack could use. He gripped the torn edge and heaved desperately.

"Hold him off!" he cried to the others.

Ruby raked Bortus with her fire-beams, leaving a dark charred scar across his skin. Their enemy gritted his teeth as smoke rose from his wounds, but when it cleared, he looked up, unharmed. "Little scratch," he said with a silver grin.

His maces sucked back into his arms and his hands lengthened into serrated blades that spun like chainsaws.

Jack stepped away from the ripped panel and stationed himself in front of his friends, brandishing Blaze.

"They shouldn't have sent children to fight me," said Bortus. "I'll send you back in pieces!"

Jack jumped at him, swinging the sword. Bortus blocked and Blaze lodged in the spinning saw-blade with a horrible grinding sound. With one hand on the hilt, he drove his other golden fist into Bortus's jaw. The brute's head jerked sideways, but then returned to the centre. Jack shook out his hand – it was like punching a wall.

"You've got a good left hook, kid," said Bortus. "My turn!"

He brought his chainsaw hand down in a vertical cut, and Jack reached up to grab his enemy's wrist. They locked together, the sword on one saw, while Jack used his strength to hold off the other. Bortus was strong, and as he pressed with his massive weight, Jack saw his silvered skin shimmering with

Xanthrum power.

Maybe he'll run out soon ... I might be able to wear him down. His hands glowed golden as he directed all his power into them.

But Bortus lifted up a foot and kicked Jack hard in the stomach. He

flew backwards in a heap. Standing triumphantly, Bortus returned his hands to normal, and he pressed the button on his wrist again for another surge of energy.

"We're almost out!" called Ruby from behind. Sure enough, she was using her fire-beams like lasers to cut a larger opening in the pod's wall. A section fell away, revealing the jungle clearing on the other side.

"Going somewhere?" said Bortus. His hands became club-shaped, like metal baseball bats.

Danny went through the gap first, followed by Ruby. As Bortus rushed them, raising his club-hands, Jack dived through too.

"There's no way he'll fit," said Ruby. "It was barely big enough for us to—"

Bortus smashed through the wall like a wrecking ball.

"You were saying?" Danny said. He belted out a supersonic blast and the force of it lifted Bortus off his feet and hurled him back into the wreckage.

"We can keep him busy!" said Ruby, following up with fire-beams that collapsed more of the pod on top of their enemy. "Find my mum, Jack!"

Jack didn't like leaving his friends, but he could see their abilities gave

them the best chance of keeping Bortus at a distance.

"I will!" he said. "Good luck, guys!"

He ran back to where he'd seen Dr Jabari, but there was no sign of her, or her masked captor.

"Hawk, can you track them?" he said.

"I sense heat signatures at a distance of fifty metres."

The Oracle extended an infrared filter over Jack's eye and, sure enough, he saw two figures off to his right. He raced in that direction, crashing through the foliage. The targets were stationary, and as he closed in, he slowed. Their voices reached his ears through the trees.

"Where is the compass?" asked the grave-voiced man.

"I've told you ..." Ruby's mother sounded desperately weak. "I don't know what you're talking about."

Jack stepped with care, flicking aside

the infrared filter as he neared Dr Jabari and her questioner.

"You're lying," said their enemy. From their shadows, Jack saw he held the back of Dr Jabari's head in one hand, even as she struggled. "We have your reports. We know the ancients left a compass to find the weapon the inscription on the stone tablet speaks of. It is hidden, in pieces, in sacred sites in this jungle. What else does the inscription say?"

"I ... I won't tell you anything," said Dr Jabari.

"Very well," said her captor. Jack saw him drawing his Xanthrum injector from under his robes with his free hand and bringing it towards Dr Jabari's face. "Then I'm afraid you are of no more use to me ..."

"No, please, I can't take any more ..."

Jack burst from the trees, swinging Blaze at the silver-masked stranger. The villain raised the arm holding the canister gun and Jack's weapon glanced off the gauntlet. Hurling Dr Jabari away, the man jetted back up into the trees. Jack reached out to grab his ankle, but his fingertips closed a fraction too late, on nothing. His enemy vanished into the canopy.

Jack dropped to Dr Jabari's side.

Ruby's mum was lying on the ground, moving weakly. Her skin was covered in a sheen of sweat, and almost seemed to gleam a pale metallic colour. With a jolt of horror, Jack realised she wasn't just injured, but ill.

"I've been poisoned," she told him. "The Agent has contaminated me with Xanthrum."

The Agent? So that was the name of the mastermind.

"How do we cure you?" asked Jack.

Dr Jabari shook her head. "You mustn't worry about me now. The important thing is to stop him before he uncovers the weapon."

"What is the weapon?"

Her eyes widened, and Jack turned to see a huge tree trunk, sharpened to a stake, flying straight towards them. Jack scooped up Dr Jabari and hurled himself away, just as the point of the trunk gouged a deep hole in the earth.

The next moment, Bortus emerged through the trees, another sapling in one hand while he used his chainsaw appendage to sharpen its tip. Then he hoisted it over his shoulder like a javelin. With nowhere to go, Jack raised his hand in a feeble gesture.

We're finished.

BORTUS LAUNCHED the enormous stake, but just before it impaled Jack something made it veer off target and crunch into the tree behind them. Jack, confused for a moment, saw Danny, his hands on either side of his mouth. Now he understood.

He used a sonic blast to send it off target!

An angry growl emerged from Bortus's throat. Danny cried out again, and knocked the muscled thug on to his back.

Perhaps the brute is finally weakening ...

Ruby must have sensed it too, because she fired a beam of flames into the canopy above their enemy. Branches and leaves tumbled down on top of Bortus. Ruby didn't let up, using her weapons to bring down more and more foliage.

"Go, Ruby!" said Danny. "Bury him!"

Jack turned his attention back to Dr Jabari. "Can you stand?" he asked.

"I don't think so," she replied. She cast a glance towards the pile of branches where Bortus had fallen. "Is he—"

From the pile of vegetation came the sound of a chainsaw, and a spinning blade emerged. Bortus burst free of his prison looking angrier than ever, his eyes almost solid silver. He was pressing the button on his wrist again, giving himself another boost of Xanthrum.

Then he cricked his neck from side to side. "Now, where were we?"

"He's invincible!" muttered Danny. "Unless we can cut off his Xanthrum supply, we've got no chance."

Jack swallowed. His friend was right. Even Blaze barely made a dent in the metal-powered man.

But there might be another way ...

"Remember what happened to the snake," he said. "It had too much Xanthrum. Maybe we can overload Bortus too?"

Their enemy's hands were morphing back into wedge-shaped anvils, each one big enough to make a horrible mess if it connected with a human body. But Jack's eyes were on the button on Bortus's wrist.

I have to get close ...

"Cover me, guys," he said, and set off at a run deeper into the jungle, hearing Bortus chuckling behind him.

"Your little Hero friend is running away!"

Jack heard Danny let rip a sonic cry at Bortus, and flames crackled from Ruby's eyes. He took that as his cue to veer back. He hadn't really been running away – he just needed the element of surprise. When he came back into view, Bortus's body was moving jerkily as he fought against energy bolts and fire-beams, but managing to press closer to the others. With all his focus on them, he didn't see Jack coming at all.

Jack jumped through the air, sending power to his hands, and landed on Bortus's back. The giant grunted, forgetting about Danny and Ruby, and lifted his club-hands to snatch blindly at Jack. Before they could grab hold, Jack leant over and grabbed the button on the giant's wrist, pressing it and holding it in. He felt the pulse of the Xanthrum coursing through Bortus's veins.

"Get off me!" roared the former Academy student.

His hands morphed again, into drillbits, then swords and saws, spikes and dagger-like forks. Jack fought them off with his free arm, all the time keeping the button down

to flood Bortus with the metalloid fluid. And it was working! Bortus's movement became more sluggish, as his limbs were being weighed down. Then he stumbled and fell to one knee.

"Get ... off ... me ..." he said, his voice drawn-out and deep, like a recording played at half speed.

Gradually the hands stopped moving at all, and Jack felt Bortus's torso stiffen beneath him. The silver gleam spread over his entire body as he fell completely still. Jack slid off, finally letting the button go.

Danny approached slowly, a frown

on his face, then lowered his bow. He poked at Bortus's face with a finger and their enemy remained motionless, a Xanthrum statue.

"You did it," he said.

Jack looked into the criminal's silvered eyes, wondering if he saw anything at all. Bortus's metal teeth were set in a mad, shining grimace. "His strength was his weakness too," he said. Glancing round, he felt a tingle of unease. "Where's Ruby?"

"She's up here," said a voice.

They all looked up, Dr Jabari included.

The Agent was floating above them

with his jetpack firing, maybe six metres up, clutching Ruby in front of his body in one hand. In the other, he held what looked like a book. Jack used Hawk to zoom in, and saw it was actually the pale stone tablet from the Taah Lu temple.

"Let her go!" shouted Danny.

"Really?" said the Agent. "All right, if you insist."

And he released his grip.

Ruby screamed as she fell, only for her captor to catch her again by one arm. Jack's heart was in his mouth as his friend dangled above the forest floor. If she fell, she'd break her back for certain.

"What do you want?" Jack asked.

"I thought that was clear," said the Agent. "'I need the compass to find a weapon. I believe the inscription on this tablet contains instructions." His gaze flicked to Dr Jabari. "You wouldn't tell me before, but I think you may be reconsidering now."

"Don't tell him, Mum!" cried Ruby.

The Agent swung her back and forth menacingly, then threw her into the air before catching her by one ankle. Danny covered his face, unable to watch.

Jack saw that Dr Jabari was even

more distraught. “All right! All right!” she said. “The inscription says the compass is in three parts. The first is within the stone tablet itself. It is said that each of the fragments will lead you to the next one.”

The Agent’s face was impossible to read under the mask, but he looked at the stone tablet in one hand and then Ruby in the other.

He let go of her again, and this

time he made no effort to catch her.

Dr Jabari screamed as her daughter dropped like a stone.

Jack lurched forwards, barely reaching Ruby before she hit the ground. Catching her as best he could, he cushioned her impact just enough to keep her from getting badly hurt. They both collapsed in a heap on the jungle floor.

"Thanks!" said Ruby. "Are you all right?"

Jack could hardly breathe. The impact had knocked the wind from his lungs. But he managed a nod. Hovering above them still, the Agent took out something like a pen, and directed it at the stone tablet. A laser cut through the stone easily, and as the pieces crumbled to the ground, he was left holding what looked like a shard of aquamarine metal. It was unlike any material Jack had ever seen before, and bore no resemblance to a compass at all.

"Beautiful, isn't it?" said the Agent, rotating the piece in his fingers.

His six *fingers!* Jack realised. *Like the strange people depicted on the stone tablet itself.*

The Agent looked down at them, and though he wore a mask, Jack saw triumph in his enemy's eyes. "I have what I need."

He slid the piece of the compass inside his robes, and then shot skywards. In mere seconds, he'd vanished completely.

"Where did he go?" asked Danny.

Ruby was already at her mother's side, cradling Dr Jabari's head. "Mum, stay with us. Tell me what's wrong!"

"We need to get her to a hospital," said Jack. "She's got Xanthrum poisoning."

"There's nothing you can do," mumbled Dr Jabari.

"There must be!" said Ruby, tears welling in her orange eyes.

"Listen to me, all of you," said Dr Jabari, her gaze suddenly fierce. "The Agent is your priority now. He is not a human, and he cares nothing for humanity."

"He's an alien?" asked Danny.

"No – not quite. He is one of a subterranean people that the Taah Lu fought off five thousand years ago. He is here for revenge. Against us. And if we do not stop him getting his hands on the weapon it will be ..." She sagged back, coughing. "It will be the end of the world as we know it."

Jack looked at his friends' faces. They'd taken on plenty of threats before, and always overcome them. But this felt different. They were on their own, in the middle of the jungle, and the enemy squaring up against them was strange and terrifying indeed.

Jack put his hand on Dr Jabari's. She didn't even flinch at his strange, scaled skin. So far, his superpower, and those of his friends, had rescued him more times than he could remember. But would it be enough this time?

It has to be ...

"We'll stop him," said Jack. "That's a promise."

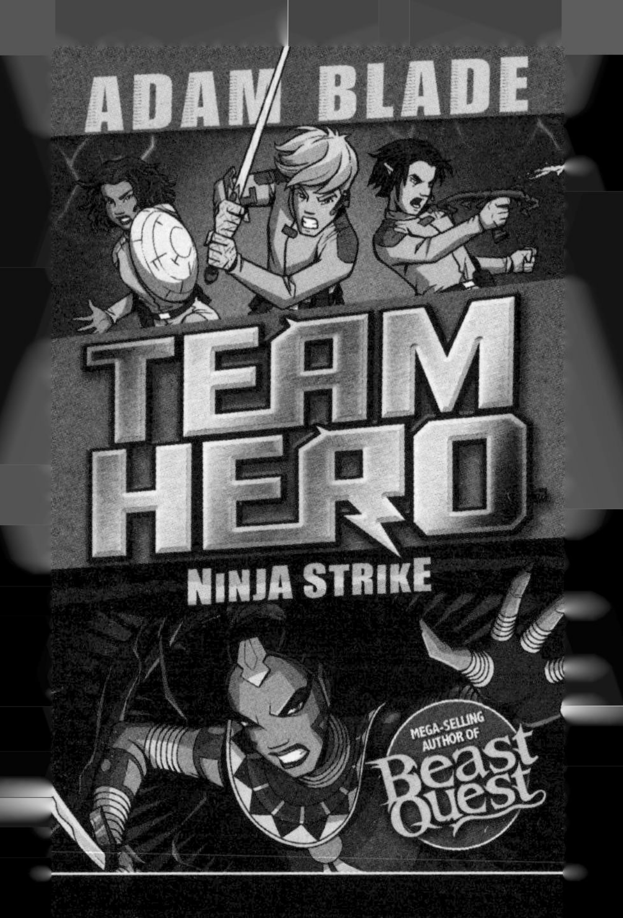

READ ON FOR A SNEAK PEEK AT BOOK 14:

CHAPTER 1

X MARKS THE SPOT

"THERE HAS to be something you can do to help her!" Ruby said, speaking to the flickering image of Professor Rufus projected above her mother's camp bed. Standing behind Ruby in the half darkness of the ruined jungle temple, Jack and Danny exchanged anxious glances. Even Jack could see Dr Jabari's condition was going downhill fast. Their enemy, the Agent, had poisoned her with a strange liquid metal called Xanthrum. Now, in the pale light filtering through tangled vines, Jack could see her skin and eyes had taken on a greyish tinge. Despite the jungle air being stiflingly hot, her whole body shivered and her skin felt cold to the touch.

Dr Jabari's eyes flickered open and she lifted a hand as if to calm her daughter. Even that effort seemed too much for her. She quickly let her fall, her eyes rolling closed.

"Please!" Ruby begged Rufus,

wringing her hands.

Professor Rufus shook his head, his freckled face lined with sorrow. "The data your Oracles have sent us regarding this metal doesn't fit with anything we know," he said. "In fact, it makes no sense at all. Our only hope of finding a cure is to locate the Agent. If we had a pure sample of the metal or if—"

The communication channel crackled suddenly and zigzag lines distorted Rufus's face. A moment later, his image vanished, leaving them staring at a crumbling wall.

Check out the next book:
NINJA STRIKE
to find out what happens next!

IN EVERY BOOK OF TEAM HERO SERIES FOUR there is a special Power Token. Collect all four tokens to get an exclusive Team Hero Club pack. The pack contains everything you and your friends need to form your very own Team Hero Club.

MEMBERSHIP CARDS • MEMBERSHIP CERTIFICATE • STICKERS • POWER GAME • BOOKMARKS

Just fill in the form below, send it in with your four tokens and we'll send you your Team Hero Club Pack.

SEND TO: Team Hero Club Pack Offer, Hachette Children's Books, Marketing Department, Carmelite House, 50 Victoria Embankment, London, EC4Y 0DZ.

CLOSING DATE: 31st December 2019

WWW.TEAMHEROBOOKS.CO.UK

Please complete using capital letters *(UK and Republic of Ireland residents only)*

FIRST NAME

SURNAME

DATE OF BIRTH

ADDRESS LINE 1

ADDRESS LINE 2

ADDRESS LINE 3

POSTCODE

PARENT OR GUARDIAN'S EMAIL

I'd like to receive Team Hero email newsletters and information about other great Hachette Children's Group offers (I can unsubscribe at any time)

Terms and conditions apply. For full terms and conditions please go to teamherobooks.co.uk/terms

TEAM HERO Club packs available while stocks last. Terms and conditions apply.

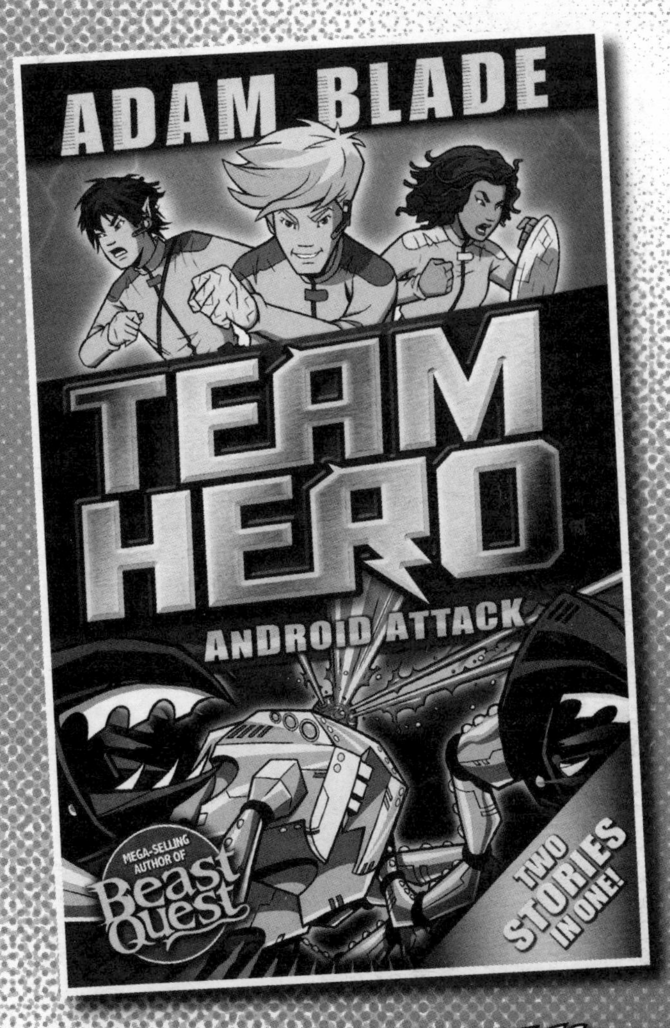

FIND THIS SPECIAL BUMPER BOOK ON SHELVES NOW!

Ring 18/01/19